Wizards and Wampum

Legends of the Iroquois

Wizards and Wampum

Legends of the Iroquois

Retold by Roger Squire
Illustrated by Charles Keeping

ABELARD-SCHUMAN

London New York Toronto

© *Copyright 1972, text by Roger Squire*
pictures by Charles Keeping

"Turtle on the War-Path" and
"Turkey's Brother Goes in Search of a Wife"
based on the book SENECA INDIAN MYTHS
by Jeremiah Curtin. © *Copyright 1923 by E. P. Dutton & Co., Inc.*
Renewal © *1951 by J. Curtin Cardell.*
Published by E. P. Dutton & Co.,
Inc. and reprinted with their permission.

Library of Congress Catalogue Card Number: 71-156584
ISBN: 0 200 71819 3 Trade
*   0 200 71820 7 GB*
Published on the same day in Canada
by Abelard-Schuman Canada Limited

LONDON
Abelard-Schuman
Limited
8 King St.
WC2

NEW YORK
Abelard-Schuman
Limited
257 Park Ave. So.
10010

TORONTO
Abelard-Schuman
Canada Limited
228 Yorkland Blvd.
425

An Intext Publisher
Printed in the United States of America

To my father

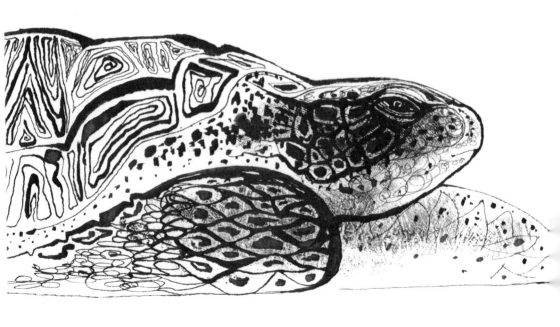

Contents

Introduction

The land of the Iroquois in upper New York State was ideal for the support of Indian civilization. The dense woods, the open meadows, and the hills and valleys, lying between the Hudson River on the east and the Genesee River on the west, were rich with moose, elk, bear, deer, raccoons and rabbits. The many small lakes, rivers and creeks were filled with fish, and from the fertile soil came dependable crops of corn, squash and beans. The land trails could be traveled in all seasons, and the many waterways made it possible to traverse the vast area bordered by the Great Lakes and the St. Lawrence River on the north, the Atlantic Ocean on the east, and the Mississippi River on the west.

With these advantages the five tribes of the Iroquois conquered all the nearby tribes in the seventeenth century and sent raiding parties as far west as the Mississippi River and as far south as Tennessee and the Carolinas. Had the Europeans not arrived with their superior weapons, they eventually might have developed this territory into a great empire.

Strong and intelligent, the Iroquois were a happy people, advanced in religion and government. The League of the Five Nations, which included the Senecas, Onondagas, Oneidas, Cayugas and Mohawks, was founded in the middle of the sixteenth century to promote the well-being of its members. Each tribe or nation was like a state and was represented at the great councils by its *sachems* or leaders. It is said that the Iroquois form of government was used as a model for the Constitution of the United States.

Each tribe was divided into clans, consisting of a number of families related by blood through the female side. Each family (all the living male and female descendants of a woman) lived in a comfortable, rectangular longhouse made of poles and elm bark. The men built the longhouse, made the tools, hunted the game and protected the village from its enemies. The women cultivated the fields, took care of the home, made the clothing and helped rule the tribe. The older women elected the chiefs from among the eligible men, and the women chose wives and husbands for their children.

The Iroquois believed in a Great Spirit who ruled the world with the help of many lesser spirits, and they gave thanks to Him through the six great festivals which took place at important periods of the year. The first, the Maple Festival, came early in the spring when the maple sap, their chief source of sweetening, began to flow. This was followed by the Planting Festival, the Wild Strawberry Festival, the Green Corn Festival, the Harvest Festival and the Midwinter Festival which celebrated the coming of the New Year.

They also believed in magic and that any person could become possessed by an evil spirit and be turned into a wizard or witch. They were convinced that animals could think and talk the way human beings did and humans could turn themselves into animals. They thought stone giants came down from the north and that pygmies lived beneath waterfalls and in the earth. One of the main forms of entertainment was listening to the tales of such strange and wonderful creatures told on a winter's night around the longhouse fire.

Although the Iroquois were skillful orators and interesting storytellers, they never developed a written language. Their treaties were preserved in pictures woven into wampum belts made of shells. Their stories and necessary records were kept in their memories.

Today most of the Iroquois live on reservations set aside for them years ago by the United States Government. Some have kept their old religion; some have adopted Christianity. Some have remained farmers; some have acquired trades in the city.

It is hoped that these stories, inspired by ancient legends, but freely adapted for children, will indicate the richness of the Iroquois imagination.

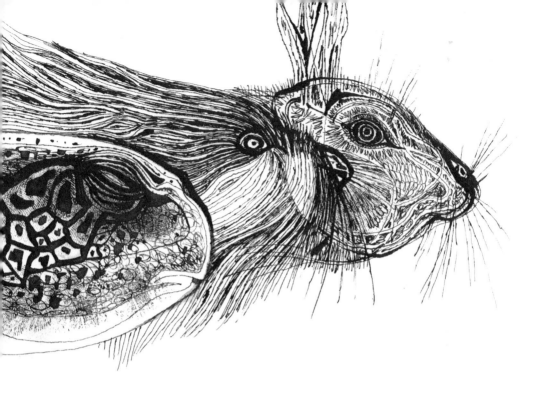

Feather Toes

Many years ago the five tribes of the Iroquois hunted in peace among the lakes and rivers and deep forests of New York. The Senecas were the largest of these tribes, with villages scattered through the rich valley of the Genesee River.

In the village of Nonda there lived a boy who had no mother or father and only one impatient uncle to take care of him. He was a big boy, but slow in thinking, with awkward hands and feet.

"How can I teach you to hunt when you can't pull a bow quickly enough to hit a porcupine?" his uncle exclaimed angrily one day. "And you are always watching the sky instead of the trail! Why don't you go and live there? Perhaps an eagle will feed you!"

The boy returned to the village sadly and lay down to watch a hawk soar upon a rising stream of air. If only he too had wings! How wonderful it would be to go each day on an adventure with the great sun spirit and then at night cover himself with a blanket of stars!

Again and again as the days went by, he would leap into

the air and beat his arms hopefully. But his body was too heavy with flesh and bones to rise.

The people laughed at his clumsy attempts to fly. At the age of fourteen when it was time for him to be given a man's name, they called him Feather Toes.

To get nearer the sky he loved he built himself a little house of bark and branches in the tallest oak upon the tallest hill nearby. And there he was, high among the leaves, on the afternoon he fell asleep and had the dream which finally freed him from the earth.

He dreamed that he met an old, old man whose eyes had seen the happenings of a thousand years. "I have been waiting for you," the old man said. "Where do you hide when I send the wind?"

"What message has the wind for me?" Feather Toes asked. "I have no magic. I have no wings."

The old man rose slowly into the air. "Put aside all fear," he said, "and follow me."

When Feather Toes opened his eyes, he felt as light as milkweed down. He walked to the end of a limb, threw himself forward, and went floating off into the air. At last, at last he was free!

He wet his face upon a drifting scarf of clouds and matched wings against an eagle scanning the earth for prey. Then a sudden wind caught him up with such force that his beating arms were no stronger against it than the wings of a maple seed. Far up the valley of the Genesee the wind carried him and dropped him upon a great cliff which jutted out into the river three hundred paces below.

Had the old man summoned the wind? Feather Toes wondered. He stepped to the edge of the cliff and gazed down at the river, a lazy band of brown and green. Though his feet were firmly on the ground, he still had the wonderful feeling of flight. Nearby was a tree heavy with plums. And a short walk revealed edible roots and plants and signs of small game.

"Here is where I shall live," he said to himself, "when I am not in the sky."

That evening as he sat on the edge of the cliff, his thoughts were brought down from the clouds by a voice such as would come from the depths of a mountain. "Give me some corn," it said.

Feather Toes was frightened. He stepped out into the air and looked for an opening in the earth from which the voice might have come. He found none. But when he had studied the unbroken walls on each side of the river, he noticed that his cliff rose from below in the shape of a man's face, a very old face and very wise. Returning to the grass, he threw a handful of corn over the edge.

19 FEATHER TOES

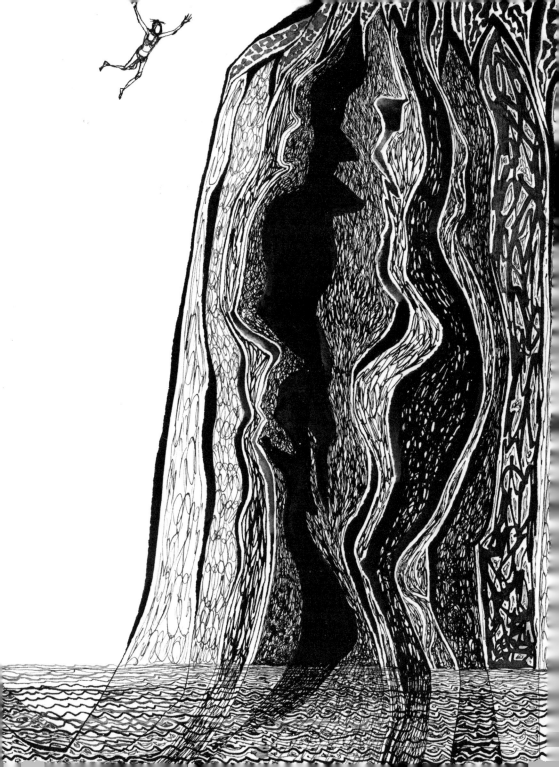

"Here is your corn, Grandfather," he said.

"Thank you," the voice replied. "It was my wind that brought you here."

Feather Toes then recognized the voice as that of the old man in his dream. "For what purpose did you bring me?" he asked. "I am slow upon the earth, helpless against the wind in the sky."

"The great hunters may have better ears for a wolf or a deer," the old man said, "but you have better ears for words. So I have brought you to my cliff to share with you the tales I still carry in my heart. If you will listen well and take them back to your people, you will live out your days with all the rewards of a chief."

Feather Toes flew down to a smooth rock beside the water and sat as still as the moss at his feet. "I am listening," he said.

"Long, long ago," the old man began, "there was a race of little folk who lived in caves behind the waterfalls."

Feather Toes shut out all other sounds and tried to remember every word that came forth from the cliff. It was a tale such as he had never heard before. How brave and wise the little folk were! When it was finished, he felt that he could still hear their voices singing in the night.

Each evening for two moons the old man told Feather Toes

a tale of ancient times. Each morning Feather Toes repeated it almost word for word to the silent cliff. His mind now was like a barren meadow which spring had sown with flowers.

Then all too soon a scouting party of frost spirits came down from the north with their white nets and put an end to the freedom of summer. The old man withdrew into the warm earth and spoke no more.

Feather Toes returned to his fire, heavy at heart and in body as well. He had been given wings to be brought to this cliff, but now he could no longer fly. He gathered a pouchful of hickory nuts and fruit and set out along the river, which he knew would eventually take him to a village or fishing lodge. How slow his feet seemed! And yet as he stumbled over the rocks and stones, he did not feel sad. In his thoughts he could still fly from one adventure to another beyond the control of frost or time.

As he settled beneath a maple tree for his first night, he heard the cry of a panther only a little distance away. To his ears, it sounded familiar. Could it be the huge male panther who had killed two of his cousins? The panther was savage and quick and strong, feared by everyone in the village.

The cry came nearer. Then Feather Toes was frightened. He had met no game in the area. The panther must have picked up his trail! And here he was without a dagger, a spear or a bow and arrow. He climbed the maple tree quietly, knowing that the panther could climb as well as he. Then he tried to pierce the darkness with his ears and eyes. At last he heard the whisper of moving leaves and saw a great paw against the trunk of his tree. How could be defend himself?

Suddenly one of the old man's tales came to mind.

"Are you the panther who ate my father?" he asked.

Panther was surprised. "No," he said, "I'm not. But I'm going to eat your father's son."

"That's wonderful!" Feather Toes exclaimed. "I'll come right down and save you the trouble of climbing the tree."

Panther was further surprised. "Do you mean that you would enjoy being eaten?" he asked.

"Of course!" Feather Toes replied. "My father and I are wizards, not men. We can make ourselves as little as we please, and no tooth or claw can harm us. In your stomach I would be warmer than here in this tree and I wouldn't have to hunt my own food or build a home. I might even stay all winter!"

Panther withdrew his paw from the trunk.

"Would you like to hear about my father's adventure before you eat me?" Feather Toes went on.

"Yes," Panther said. "It might be a very good idea."

Feather Toes raised his voice. "My father was sleeping one

night in the forest," he began, "when your uncle or your cousin came upon him and attacked him. My father could have become invisible or killed the panther with a magic word. But he had never been eaten before and thought it might be an interesting experience.

"So when he reached your uncle's stomach—if it was your uncle—he pulled himself together and looked around. It was a little small for running a race, which my father loved to do, but warm and comfortable. So he decided that he would make it his home for a while. He locked up the door that led out of the stomach, to avoid a draft, and sat down to smoke his pipe. How pleasant it was!

"Your uncle, however, was not happy to have such a guest. He found that he was just as hungry after he had eaten my father as he had been before. So he went hunting again and pretty soon caught a rabbit. When my father saw the rabbit come in through the roof of his new home, he was even more pleased. His meals apparently were going to be free. He roasted the meat over a small fire until it was tender and ate every bit.

"By this time your uncle was wondering what had gone wrong. The more he ate, the hungrier he got. And why did he feel so warm? Why was smoke coming out of his nose and mouth? He was frightened.

25 FEATHER TOES

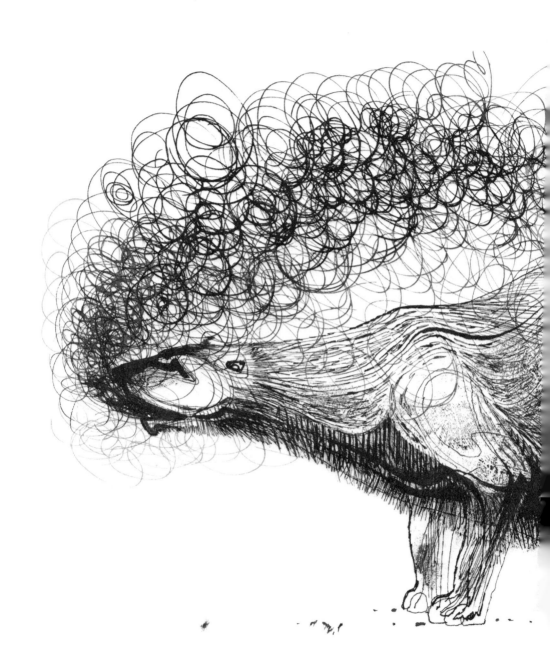

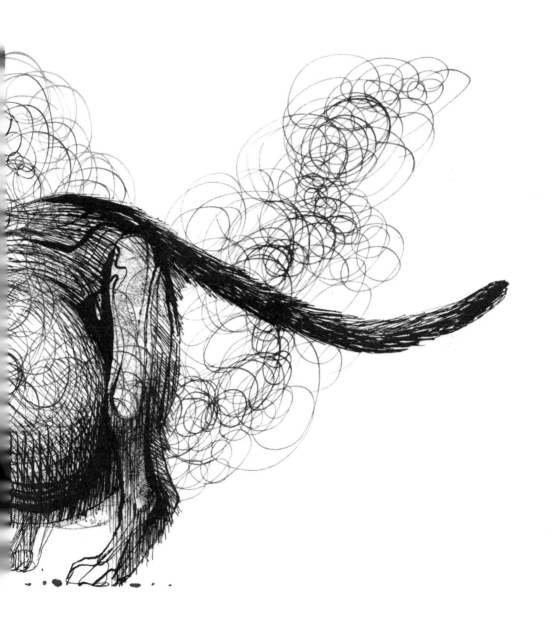

"Well, this went on for about five days. Your uncle became so weak that he could hardly hunt. And when this happened, of course my father didn't eat so well. Besides he was getting tired of nothing but meat. So on the sixth day he flew out of your uncle's mouth and went home and cooked himself a great big bowl of corn pudding.

"Never again, your uncle promised himself, would he eat another wizard!

"But little did he know about wizards.

"When my father had finished his pudding, he found your uncle again and said to him, 'Will you please open your mouth so I can come back home?'

" 'I will not!' your uncle replied. 'I've had more than enough of you!'

"But the moment he opened his mouth, quick as a hummingbird, my father leaped down his throat. And there he was, all snug again with a nice fat woodchuck prepared for dinner.

"Your uncle drank almost half a pond of water to drown him. He ate dry grass to smother him, until his stomach looked like a giant puffball. He stood on his head and shook himself until he was dizzy.

"Nothing worked. And I myself would have been born in your uncle's stomach if my mother hadn't wanted to live beside a garden. So one fine spring day my father opened your uncle's mouth from the inside and returned to his village, never to see your uncle again.

"That is the end of the tale."

There was silence. Feather Toes waited. Still Panther did not speak.

"I'm coming down now," Feather Toes called. "It's getting cold up here, and I would like a nice warm home for the winter."

When his feet touched the ground, he found that he was alone. Laughing to himself, he lay down beside his fire and went to sleep. He had lost the magic of wings, but had gained the magic of words.

In the morning he went on, to the north. Perhaps he could bring all animals under control with his tales, but what about people? And how was he to live? How was he to eat and build a home and find a woman who would marry him? He decided to follow the old man's example and try to trade each tale for a gift of corn.

When he stepped through the stockade of the first village, he was quickly surrounded by several older men and women and a number of excited children.

"Do you come from afar?" the oldest woman asked.

"Yes," Feather Toes replied. "I am a teller of tales, and I

will tell you many adventures from the ancient times if you are willing to listen. But first I must have some corn."

"If your tongue is well sweetened," the woman said, "you are welcome among us and will not lack for corn."

Feather Toes sat upon the ground. His audience formed half a circle in front of him. He began in a gentle voice.

And these are some of the tales he told.

Moving Day

Turtle forced his eyes open and thrust his head slowly out from his shell to see whether the night had been cold enough to rim his pond with frost. The earth, he found, was still untouched. The sun was late and weak, however, and the brook murmured drowsily as it tumbled over the last bed of rock before reaching the pond. It was time to be thinking about his long winter's sleep.

Suddenly he was no longer content with his way of life. Why did he have to crawl into the mud each autumn and stay there till spring, locked in a silent prison? Why couldn't he have a winter home as nice as some of his friends?

There was Squirrel, for example. What a wonderful nest he had high in the butternut tree! Inside its leafy walls he was safe and comfortable, with enough room to move around in as well.

Turtle decided that when the sun had warmed him a little, he would ask Squirrel to help him build as pleasant a home upon the ground.

He found his friend clinging to the far end of a branch with his wife scolding him from the other.

"May I ask you about a problem?" Turtle said.

"Gladly!" Squirrel replied. "Gladly!" He jumped to another tree and ran down its trunk.

"And don't you dare go off anywhere without fixing it!" his wife called after him.

"What's the trouble?" Turtle asked with sympathy.

"She says I didn't build our house right and she has a stiff neck from the draft!" Squirrel grumbled. "I wish she had a stiff jaw too! Then she couldn't complain so much! What's wrong with you?"

"I was just wishing that I had a winter home like yours," Turtle admitted. "But I guess yours isn't perfect, either."

"Far from it!" Squirrel exclaimed. "My wife and I can't get away from each other! If I had a nice big house like Raccoon's, I could live inside one branch and my wife inside another. I could store my seeds and nuts in it, too, so I wouldn't have to go out in the cold to get something to eat!"

"If Raccoon should give it up for any reason," Turtle said, "why couldn't you live in the branches and I live down among the roots?"

Then they looked at each other and smiled.

"If I had your brain," Squirrel said, "I could find a reason why he should give it to us."

"And if I had your gift of speech," Turtle told him, "I would know how to talk him into it."

"Then let's work together," Squirrel suggested, "and see what we can do."

"Fine!" said Turtle. "That tree doesn't look very safe to me."

Squirrel laughed. "I'll make him think it's going to fall over tomorrow!" he said.

So off they went that evening to the old maple in which Raccoon lived the year round. It was a splendid home for anyone, with three hollow branches and a huge, partly hollow trunk.

"Good evening," Squirrel called.

Raccoon, who had just awakened, looked out his window. "Welcome!" he exclaimed. He thought that Squirrel was his friend. Besides he was as polite as he was tidy. "Welcome to you both!"

"Your house is what we want to talk to you about," Squirrel explained. "Turtle is so worried that he asked me to come over and see you."

Raccoon studied both Squirrel and Turtle carefully. He was wiser than they thought. He could have been chief of all the raccoons if he had wanted to. Surely they didn't know that only last night he had found a dangerous crack on the thin

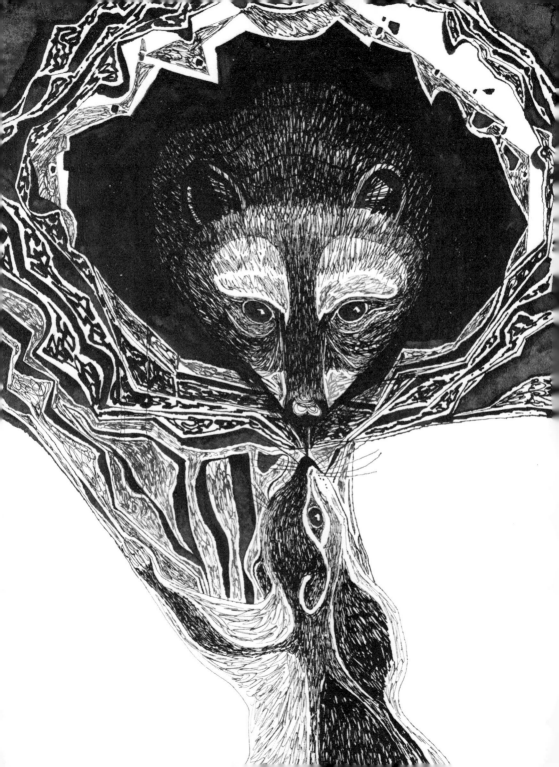

side of the trunk and had picked out a new home? He decided that they were up to something. He decided to play as innocent as they.

"I'm very grateful for your interest," he said to Turtle. "What do you think is wrong with it?"

"Don't you know," Squirrel said, "that Bear chose this tree as his home but never moved in because he was sure that it would be blown down by the first bad winter wind?"

Raccoon pretended to be worried. "No," he said. "He didn't tell me that."

"Why don't you let me examine the different parts," Squirrel offered, "and find out whether it's safe?"

Raccoon remembered that the crack did not show through the bark. "The children are still asleep," he said. "But if you could do it from the outside, that would be fine, although I'm afraid I can't pay you very much."

This was a new thought to Squirrel. He had not expected to be paid. But what harm would it do to earn a little present by his trickery as well as a new home?

"Oh, I wouldn't demand a payment from a friend," he said. "But of course it will take a lot of time and careful thought. So if you happen to know where you could get—let's say, about twenty walnuts or hickory nuts, it would keep my wife a little quieter."

35 MOVING DAY

Raccoon did happen to know where there were twenty walnuts—right in one of Squirrel's own hiding places, which he had discovered by accident three days ago. And he saw no reason why he should pay Squirrel to look at a house which he was going to give up.

"Very well," he answered, "I'll deliver that number of walnuts when you have finished the job."

Squirrel leaped up onto a stump happily. Then he studied Raccoon's tree from its crown to its roots, jerking his tail up and down as he did when he was excited. "I certainly didn't think it was that bad!" he exclaimed.

"Bad in what way?" Raccoon asked.

"Look at it!" Squirrel exclaimed. "It even leans toward the south. So when the north wind blows, it already has a head-start to the ground."

"Oh, dear!" said Raccoon. "And it has such lovely storage space."

Squirrel climbed down solemnly. "I'll do what repair work I can," he offered, "so it won't fall down right away. But I can't promise anything without charging you more nuts."

"If I could get some help," Raccoon asked, "wouldn't it be much safer to move?"

At this Squirrel almost laughed out loud. "It might be," he agreed. "Yes, it might. But where will you get the help?"

Raccoon was pretty sure that Squirrel had stored other pockets of nuts near the first one. So he made a new offer.

"I know a tree that might do," he said. "But I want a separate nest for every member of the family. Your teeth are sharper than mine. I'll give you twice the number of walnuts if you'll chew the nests out for me."

"I think I could," said Squirrel happily.

"And it would be much easier to do," Raccoon said, "if someone would take care of the children while my wife and I are making the beds more comfortable with grass and ferns."

"I will make the new rooms," Squirrel said. "And Turtle and I will take turns watching the babies."

Then Squirrel and Turtle said good-bye and left. All three were pleased with the bargain.

Turtle, however, was not quite as pleased as Squirrel. "What good will twenty nuts do me?" he asked. "Why didn't you demand ten nuts and ten fish?"

"Because I'm doing most of the work," Squirrel said, "and I don't like fish."

"You *should* do most of the work!" Turtle pointed out. "You will have most of the tree!"

"Let's not quarrel," Squirrel said. "We're both going to have a wonderful home for the winter."

Squirrel did not love his work. Even with his sharp teeth, it was hard to cut out four nests from living wood. And, of course, his wife scolded him for being away so much. How glad he would be when the cold weather slowed down her tongue!

Raccoon, on the other hand, was so pleased that he dug up half of Squirrel's nuts and paid him these before he was through. Then he watched where Squirrel hid them and dug them up again for his second payment.

No, it did not go well for Squirrel. When he had finished the bedrooms, it was time to sit with the babies. The young raccoons were twice as heavy as he and as playful as young foxes. They loved their new nurse.

"I get him first," exclaimed Sister.

"We'll take turns in every game!" Brother said.

"What kind of games do you want to play?" Squirrel asked.

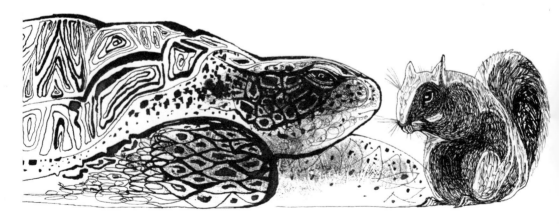

"We'll go on a war party," Brother said, "and you'll be the enemy."

"No!" exclaimed Squirrel.

But he was too late. With wild whoops the two chased him up and down inside the trunk and finally caught him near the top.

"He's our prisoner!" Brother shouted. "Torture him! Torture him!"

Sister bit Squirrel in the rear several times, playfully but hard enough to hurt, then pretended to bite his head.

"That's not fair!" Brother cried. "The man is the one who should scalp him!"

"I'll tell your father!" Squirrel exclaimed desperately.

At that very moment Raccoon looked down inside the tree and smiled to himself. "Are you having a good time, children?" he asked.

"Oh, yes, Daddy!" Brother replied, catching Squirrel's tail in his teeth. "Watch!"

"You must only pretend to torture him," Raccoon said, "and not bite off his tail. He would look queer without it."

"And you didn't pay me for that!" Squirrel added.

It was Brother who tired of the sport first—that is, after Squirrel, who had had more than enough after the first attack.

"Let's not play that game anymore," Brother said. "Let's play catch with him."

"All right," Sister agreed.

But Squirrel gave a leap beyond the reach of her paw and scampered down the trunk to the ground where Turtle was resting.

"It's your turn now," he said. "And I won't pay you in nuts, I'll pay you in fish."

They were all interrupted at this point, however, by Squirrel's wife who came scolding through the branches.

"So this is where you are!" she exclaimed to Squirrel.

"We're playing games," Brother informed her.

"Oh!" she said. Then she turned her anger upon Squirrel. "You won't even take your children for a walk! But you'll come over and waste half the day with someone else's children! You come with me right now and start to work on our winter home!"

"That's what I'm doing!" Squirrel said. "You don't understand!"

"I certainly don't!" she exclaimed. "But maybe you can understand this?" She gave Squirrel a sharp nip in the tail, which was already sore. "Now get along!" she said.

Brother and Sister waved a sad good-bye. They liked to

play with Squirrel. They hoped that Turtle would be fun to play with too.

The following afternoon, they pretended that Turtle was a canoe and rode on his back around and around the pond until he sank to the bottom, exhausted. For ten fish or a hundred fish, he told himself, he wouldn't get within range of them again!

Raccoon came to the edge of the pond several times during this merry-go-round and laughed and laughed. Altogether he was enjoying a very pleasant vacation.

Then suddenly the north wind began to moan in the distance, and came down out of the hills, fleeing before the frost spirits. "Hurry, hurry, hurry!" it moaned. "It's cold, cold, cold!"

Raccoon did not have to hurry. He was settled now in a nice warm new home, paid for in full.

Squirrel thought that he too did not have to hurry. "Now I will show you what I have been working at," he said to his wife. "You'll be sorry that you scolded me when you see our new home." With a nut in his mouth, he led her from branch to branch toward the Raccoon's tree, which was now vacant and ready to be lived in.

They had barely started, however, when they heard a great crash in its direction.

"What was that?" his wife asked.

"It sounded like a tree," he said in a voice quiet with fear.

They went on. They jumped from stone to stone across a narrow brook. They climbed a trunk to their natural paths again. Squirrel dreaded to look down. Then all too soon there was Raccoon's tree, twisted and broken, lying on the ground. Beside it lay Turtle, stunned.

"That's probably the tree we just heard," Squirrel's wife said. "Don't stop here! We must go on to our new home."

Squirrel turned about unhappily and headed back toward their nest. "That *was* our new home!" he said. "We'll have to sleep close together tonight to keep warm."

It is better to forget what his wife said.

And Turtle? He had lived a long time and knew that life held many disappointments. He recovered from the shock and went back to his pond. There he dug his way slowly into the mud.

The winter might be long. But at least he would pass it in peace.

The Boy Who Laughed

In the village of Towanda there lived an old man named Bent Leg who had known the Evil One many times. He had seen him put on war paint and attack a village with magic arrows that flew straight to their mark. He had lived through summers in which the Evil One had withheld the rain, so the corn turned brown and did not grow. He had known him to steal upon a village through the silence of winter and leave sickness in every home.

Where would he strike next? Bent Leg wondered every morning. Who would be his victim?

One autumn night when Bent Leg could not sleep, he heard a distant roar and saw the sky aglow with light that was not born of the sun. He knew that such a roar could come only from the throats of the fire demons who served the Evil One. Soon the whole valley would be in flames!

He called out a warning to the other members of his family. Then in a panic he caught up his grandson, Little Elk, and fled limping to a cave where long ago he had laid by a store of venison and parched corn. There in its depths he closed his eyes—and waited. Above him and all around him the fire burned with a hatred he had never known before. When it was safe to return to the village, the trees had dropped their leaves in ashes upon the ground and the one remaining house was black, without a roof, and silent.

Apparently no one else had escaped.

"Ai! Ai!" Bent Leg moaned. How could he build a house by himself? How could he protect Little Elk from the Evil One except by hiding him back in the cave?

The cave was deep and curved, with an open mouth half-way up the riverbank. He put Little Elk out of sight behind a net, and then sat by himself and pretended to be an old and worthless man alone with an ancient wound.

A year passed, and then another and another. The dark of evening was the only light Little Elk knew. And yet he was not unhappy. The shadows fed his imagination and took him on one adventure after another more glorious than any he could ever have known. He played games with the ants and centipedes that crawled upon the floor. He learned all that his grandfather could teach.

At last, however, there came a day when the warm and restless breeze called to him as it had never called before.

"Why is it, Grandfather," he asked, "that I feel as if my

whole body were humming a song that wants to burst through my skin into words? Why must I stay here forever in this cave? What is it like out there in the world?"

"Ask me no questions about the world," his grandfather said. "Your father was proud of his war club and bow, and your mother tried to make one little piece of land her own. Now they and the rest of the village are gone. You must stay here where you are safe until the Evil One has forgotten you."

"How long will that be?" Little Elk asked.

His grandfather shook his head sadly. "I don't know," he said. "I will take care of you as long as I can."

So Little Elk went back to his dreams for another year. But he was growing from a boy into a man, and as he grew, the cave seemed smaller and smaller. His arms wanted to pull and push. His legs wanted to run. He began to try the strength of the net while his grandfather slept, and to listen for sounds that were not made by the river or the low fire in the cave.

One day when his grandfather was out hunting rabbits and squirrels, Little Elk heard a clear thin whistle made by two falling notes as if someone were calling him. Could it be the Evil One, disguising his voice? Suddenly, he did not care.

"Hello!" he cried.

"Hello! Hello!" The cave echoed.

Then there was silence.

He sat down and tried to make other sounds with his mouth besides speech. He blew out his breath and drew it in, and suddenly made a whistle that went up and down in the happiest sounds he had ever heard. He tried it again and again until he could control the notes enough to form a song. Was this what the breeze had been urging him to do?

When he heard the call a second time, he found that he could repeat it exactly as it struck his ears. The whistle came nearer, echoed in the cave, and turned into the flutter of tiny wings a moment before the vague shape of a bird came to light upon the net.

"Who are you and where have you come from?" Little Elk cried with delight.

"My name is Chickadee and I live at the forest's edge," the bird informed him. "Who are you that you stay here in the depths of a cave?"

"I am Little Elk. My grandfather hid me here to escape from the Evil One," Little Elk explained.

"I have never met such a one," Chickadee said.

"My grandfather is wise," Little Elk told him. "He says that the Evil One is everywhere."

"There is a violet growing near the mouth of your cave," Chickadee said. "Was that planted by the Evil One?"

"I don't know what a violet is," Little Elk replied.

"Then come with me and I'll show you," Chickadee invited.

"Free me from this net," Little Elk said, "and I will come."

Chickadee pecked at the coarse twine of the net until it was no longer strong enough to hold Little Elk back, then he perched on his shoulder. Little Elk groped forward, trembling with excitement. At each bend the light grew stronger. Suddenly it struck his eyes with such force that for several moments he was blind.

Slowly he regained his sight. Beneath him flowed the Genesee, green and white in the April sun. Beyond it was a great cliff, topped with trees that were freshly washed with the more fragile greens of early spring. And there, clinging to a niche at the entrance of the cave, was a violet at the beginning of its bloom, the first flower that he had even seen.

"How beautiful it all is!" he cried.

There was so much to see, to touch, to hear! And the great sun itself, as it warmed his face, made him feel so happy and alive that he looked up at the sky and laughed aloud for the first time.

"Of all living creatures only a man can laugh," Chickadee said. "You have become a man."

Little Elk squeezed his fists tight with joy and laughed

49 THE BOY WHO LAUGHED

again. "I am a boy not a man," he said. "But I will be a man before my time."

"I must go now," Chickadee then said. "It is for you to decide how much of the world belongs to you."

"I want it all!" Little Elk cried.

"Then I will help you," Chickadee promised. "Good-bye."

As Chickadee flew across the river and up into the trees, Little Elk saw his grandfather coming up the path, dragging part of a deer that had fallen off the great cliff. How old and weak he looked! And every step seemed to give him pain.

"Go back! Go back!" his grandfather exclaimed, "before the Evil One finds out that I have saved you!"

"No, Grandfather," Little Elk replied. "How can anyone turn away from the sun once he has known its brightness and warmth? I want to learn how to hunt and be a man—and fight the Evil One!"

"Very well," his grandfather said at last. "I shan't be here to protect you much longer. I'll make you a bow and arrow, but you will have to prove that you are able to hunt."

To keep Little Elk near home the old man made him a bow which a grown man would have found hard to bend and a crooked arrow which would never hit its mark. But Little Elk was not discouraged. Day after day he strained at the bow until his muscles grew almost as hard as the wood itself, and finally he shot the arrow out of sight into the sky. But how could he ever hit a deer with it or kill a bear? He sat down one morning and whistled for Chickadee.

It was not long before his friend appeared.

"How shall I ever learn how to shoot," Little Elk asked, "with only this one arrow that won't go where I want it to?"

"I will teach you how to hit a moving target," Chickadee said. "If you learn how to aim it, even a crooked arrow will reach its mark."

He flew patiently from branch to branch again and again. Little Elk's arrow flew ahead of him and behind him at an ever smaller distance. Then one day Little Elk aimed his arrow and without thinking shot him through the breast.

"Oh, what have I done!" he cried, picking up Chickadee's limp body. Chickadee had taught him how to laugh. Now for the first time he learned how to weep.

"Don't be sad," Chickadee said. "It was meant that you should take me in your hand to your grandfather."

Then he died.

Little Elk waited until his grandfather had come home from hunting, and then held Chickadee out before him. "I shot it with my crooked arrow," he said. "Is that enough to earn me a straight one?"

On seeing Chickadee, his grandfather gave a groan. "The

51 THE BOY WHO LAUGHED

Evil One must have whispered in your ear!" he exclaimed. "How else could you have known that a chickadee is the first living thing a Seneca boy is allowed to shoot?"

"He was my friend," said Little Elk sadly. "I didn't mean to kill him."

"A hunter must kill or die himself," his grandfather said. "All birds and animals understand that."

Then he hesitated for a moment. "Very well," he agreed. "If you must go out into the world, I shall make you an arrow that will fly like an eagle to its prey."

"Thank you," Little Elk said. "With it I will kill the Evil One. Where shall I find him?"

"It will be the death of you if you try to fight him!" his grandfather exclaimed. "You mustn't even go near the deep pool in the bend of the river where he lives! He has taken on the body of a giant lizard with jaws that could snap off your arm or head!"

Little Elk was silent. He gave his grandfather no promise.

The next morning Little Elk began to explore his bright new world. Surely the sun at least was man's friend.

As he went from the valley to the hills, from rock to tree, like every other Seneca boy he learned to shoot a running rabbit, a flying grouse, a bounding deer, and finally a bear.

Then one day he decided that in spite of his grandfather's warning he would hunt the Evil One.

"He lives in a deep pool at the bend of the river," his grandfather had said. Little Elk took the lesser path which hugged the great cliff and crept over it without sound until the river turned sharply to the right.

There was the pool, filled with quiet inviting water, too deep to reveal whatever monster was living there.

"Come out of your hole, Evil One!" Little Elk cried. "I am not afraid!"

A great bubble of air rose from the hidden depths of the pool. Then the Evil One's head broke through the surface. It had a long nose like a deer, cruel eyes and teeth, and it was covered with green fish scales which no arrow could penetrate. With a roar it opened its jaws and shot flames and smoke in Little Elk's direction.

Little Elk dove through the flames into the water. There he twisted and turned too quickly for the great clumsy head to follow. Then he caught up stones from the bottom and threw them into the gaping mouth. One, two, three, four, five— each stone went part way down the Evil One's throat and then stuck, so that his long neck looked like a pod of ripened beans.

Gradually, the stones cut off his breath, and the flames

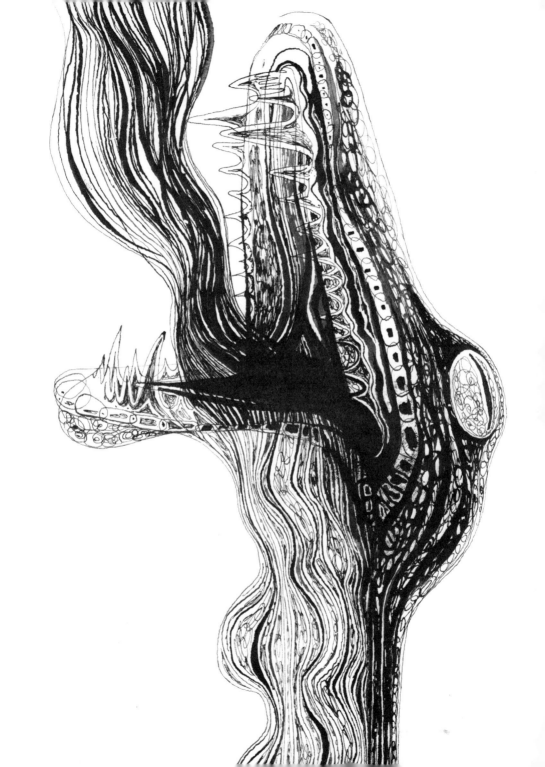

grew shorter. Finally, they were nothing but smoke, as thin and harmless as the breath of a man on a cold day. Then suddenly the neck collapsed and pulled the head back into the depths of the pool.

Little Elk stood dripping on the shore, his head tilted up to the sun, and sent his laughter echoing from cliff to cliff. He had destroyed the Evil One! He had won his first great victory! How good, how wonderful it felt!

But was the Evil One really dead? A moment before his head had disappeared, a tiny white owl had flown out of his mouth and landed on a ledge of the riverbank. It was a beautiful bird with feathers as soft as the fur of a rabbit. What a wonderful pet it would make!

Little Elk put on his clothes and went in wonder to the ledge. The owl flew a little farther. Then it kept always beyond his reach until it had led him out of the gorge. There on the edge of the woods it allowed itself to be caught.

For the rest of the day it flew back and forth over Little Elk's head or did a strange dance upon a limb. Little Elk was delighted. Then as the sun began to nibble at the tallest tree, it flew off a little distance and led him to a small bark house in a clearing. There it perched on the roof, gave a wild and weird call, and flew inside.

Who lived in this house that stood alone? Was there danger

inside? Little Elk paused at the door for a moment, then stepped into the silence that awaited him. On the bed lay a war club. He picked it up. How beautifully it was made!

The moment the war club felt the warmth of his hand, it spoke to him. "The white owl has led you to me," it said. "You are growing up. You have learned to laugh and to kill. But you won't be a man until you have learned to destroy your enemies."

"I have no enemies," Little Elk said, "except the Evil One who is now gone forever."

"You have no enemies," the war club pointed out, "because you are young and want little. But you will have to live somewhere. Wouldn't you like this house with its fields of corn and its forest rich with game?"

"Yes, I would like it," Little Elk replied. It was a good house. "But it doesn't belong to me."

"I will give it to you," the war club said, "if you will keep me in your hand and use me."

"Use you in what way?" Little Elk asked.

"You must hide in the forest tonight," the war club said, "and wait till the master has come home and gone to sleep. Then I will kill him for you and all this will be yours."

Little Elk took the war club outside and swung it over his head. Then he danced in a circle and sang a war song and

laughed again and again. With this war club he was strong! With this war club he was a man, afraid of no one! Yes, this feeling too was good.

And yet his grandfather had taught him that he must never kill another man except in defense of his own land or life. Which one was right, his grandfather or the war club? He decided to hide in the forest and see what kind of person it was who had built such a house.

That night when the fields were lighted dimly by the rising moon, he crept in silence into the house, holding his war club tightly, and found its master sleeping, his face turned toward the fire. It was a strong face, and to Little Elk it seemed a good one.

The stranger was a man like himself. He breathed as he did; slept as he did. Was he never again to wake and step out into the morning sun?

Little Elk raised his war club—and flung it into the fire. "I will have none of you!" he exclaimed. "You are just another form of the Evil One!"

The moment the war club landed in the fire, it gave a roar like that of the monster in the pool and burst in two. Out of one end flew the white owl to a position above the door.

"No!" cried Little Elk. "You will never again lead me into evil!"

The man sat up in his bed and stared at Little Elk. "Who are you," he asked, "and where did you come from?"

Little Elk told him his name. "And I have come," he said further, "from the banks of the Genesee."

"The name of my son was Little Elk," the man replied, "but he was killed in the great fire that destroyed all the people of my village except my wife and me."

"And my mother and father were killed in another great fire that spared only my grandfather and me," said Little Elk.

Then they stared at each other with hope. Could it be that all four members of their family had survived?

The man stood up and turned Little Elk's face toward the fire. "I need no proof!" he said. "You have your mother's face on the frame of a man!"

Little Elk threw himself into his father's arms. "The war club told me to kill you, but I couldn't!" he exclaimed.

"My son! My son!" his father said. "After that fire I thought I could never be happy again!"

"And my mother," Little Elk asked, "is she alive too?"

"She will be home in the morning," his father replied. "You and your grandfather, your mother and I—we'll all be together again!"

Little Elk felt more wonderful than he had ever felt before. How good it was to have a mother and father! How good it was to be alive! A flood of happiness rose in his breast and poured itself out into the night. The insects and animals all around heard a great burst of laughter such as the valley had never known before. The white owl heard it too and flew into the darkness alone.

Bear Man

Run Along put one more blackberry into his mouth. Then he parted the prickly branches carefully and stared down into a jumble of bones, cleaned and whitened by many moons of weather. Some appeared to be those of a large animal, some of a man.

As he stood there, wishing that he were not alone, a wood thrush flew down to a low branch and spoke. "I have been waiting two years for someone to find my friends," he said.

"Your friends?" Run Along asked with surprise. "Who are they?"

"One was Deer Button from your own village," Wood Thrush explained. "And the other was Bear. Each one came here for blackberries and each was afraid of the other. So as you see, they fought to the death. Will you help me now to bring them both back to life?"

"I'm not a wizard!" Run Along exclaimed. "How can I do that?"

"All you have to do is put the bones in your basket and follow me," Wood Thrush said. "I know where there is a magic spring that will grow flesh and skin upon them."

Run Along was excited. To see the bones of a skeleton grow into a living thing—how wonderful that would be!

"Very well," he said.

He was a likable but careless boy, always in a hurry, always impatient. He picked up the bones and followed Wood Thrush to the spring. It was a tiny spring that formed but one drop a day in the silent cup of stone beneath it.

"You must sprinkle the bones carefully," Wood Thrush warned. "It has taken a year for this much to gather."

Run Along laid out the two skeletons and wet them. After a moment, the bones began to move. They fastened themselves together. They covered themselves with muscles. Then one body grew light with human skin, the other dark with a coat of fur. But it was the man's body which was dark with hair, the bear's skin which was smooth and brown and presently concealed in clothes. Run Along gasped with dismay. He had put the wrong heads on the bodies, and now each was part man and part bear!

The man with the bear's head growled, then ran stumbling through the trees.

The bear with the man's head sat up slowly and spoke. "Why are you staring at me?" he asked.

"I gave you the wrong head!" Run Along exclaimed. "You're supposed to be a bear!"

Deer Button looked down at his huge paws and fur-covered body. "I don't understand!" he said. "I feel so queer!"

"You and Bear had a fight two years ago and killed each other," Run Along explained. "You feel queer because I've just brought you to life again with water from the magic spring."

"But what did you do with *my* body?" Deer Button asked.

"I brought it here along with your head," Run Along told him. "Bear just ran off with it!"

"Then you must get it back!" Deer Button said.

Run Along looked away miserably. "I can do nothing about it," he said. "There's no more water and it will take a year to fill the cup again."

Deer Button stood up like a man, took a step, then dropped to all four feet like a bear.

"But I *will* go home with you," Run Along offered. "Your wife is going to be surprised."

For once Run Along was not in a hurry. What would the villagers do to him when they saw Deer Button, now neither a man nor a bear? What would Deer Button's wife, Pudding Spoon, say to his mother?

The dogs came out through the stockade first, growling and snapping at Deer Button's legs. Then half the village, including Pudding Spoon, poured out of the longhouses, the men armed with spears and bows and arrows.

"Don't anyone shoot!" Run Along cried. "It's Deer Button come back to life again!"

Pudding Spoon stared at Deer Button with fear.

"My husband died two years ago!" she exclaimed. "This must be his ghost!"

"I'm not a ghost," Deer Button told her. "I'm alive again. The only difference is that now I'm part bear!"

"Then go home to your tree!" Pudding Spoon said. "I don't want you!"

Deer Button dropped to all four feet and took a step toward her.

"Stay where you are!" the chief shouted, aiming his spear.

Deer Button pointed one paw at Run Along. "He'll tell you what happened!" he said. "He did this to me!"

Run Along stepped between Deer Button and the chief's spear. "I can explain it all," he said reluctantly.

The people became quiet then and listened and finally accepted his story as the truth. In what other way could such a mix-up have come about?

But even the chief could not figure out how Deer Button should be treated. Was he a man or was he a bear? Or was he neither? Should he still be considered Pudding Spoon's husband or should he be made to live alone?

"The only real change," Deer Button insisted, "is that I have new clothes. That makes no difference to *me*."

Pudding Spoon spoke up then for herself. "When you slept in my bed before," she asked, "did you take off your clothes or leave them on?"

"I took them off," Deer Button replied.

"Then you can come and sleep with me only if you'll take off your new ones," Pudding Spoon said.

The chief laughed, then faced Run Along. "If Pudding Spoon won't have him," he said, "you must take him to your own longhouse for your carelessness and become his servant. You must also help him hunt food for his family."

Run Along accepted his punishment gratefully. It would be fun, he thought, to hunt with a bear that could think like a man.

But although Deer Button thought like a man, he was as clumsy and helpless as any animal. When he got into bed, his weight sent him crashing to the floor. When he tried to wash his face, he scratched it. His great paws could not hold a knife or spoon. He could not carve a dish or throw a spear or shoot a bow and arrow. Run Along found him more care than a nest of baby raccoons.

Deer Button's clumsiness, however, did not stop him from eating. Each slight drop in the temperature added to his appetite. Every day after his morning meal in the longhouse he would go out into the woods and fill his stomach with roots and nuts, and small game that he could catch or dig out of its hole. Then in the afternoon he would be hungry again. He grew fatter and fatter until he could no longer get through the longhouse door.

"You mustn't eat so *much!*" Run Along said. "What will you do when winter comes if you can't get through the door?"

Deer Button gave a tremendous yawn. "I'm not worried about winter," he said. "What I'm worried about is food. I'm hungry all the time!"

"How can you be," Run Along asked, "when you eat from morning to night?"

"Eating seems to make no difference," Dear Button said. "Let's go over to Golden Rod's house and get some of her corn pudding."

Two days later he went into the forest as usual, looking for extra food, and did not come back. The next morning Run Along tried to follow his trail, but found it covered by the first heavy snow. Being part bear, had he gone into a bear's winter sleep? Run Along wondered. Had some hunter killed him? Or had he simply eaten too much?

His concern, however, was forgotten in the reappearance

of the other half of his mistake. While looking in the snow for deer tracks, he found a trail made by the bare feet of a man. Who would be out in such weather without snowshoes or even moccasins? He hurried along the trail and found Bear, his head still attached to Deer Button's body, lying upon a bed of pine boughs. All his clothing but his breechcloth and part of one legging had either been torn off or worn to shreds, and his exposed skin was bloody and scarred. He was too weak to get up, too weak even to growl.

"Why didn't you come home to your wife?" Run Along asked with pity. "The other half of you did."

"My home is in the forest," Bear replied in a faint voice. "But I walk in the old trails like a stranger. How can I dig out a winter nest with these feeble claws, or catch food with legs no swifter than a woodchuck's?"

Run Along realized that although he had the body of a human being, he had the mind of a bear.

"Have you eaten today?" he asked.

"No," Bear replied. "Nor yesterday, nor the day before."

Run Along fed him from his pouch. Then he held out his own bearskin robe, which he had put on against the wind. Bear threw it back at him with anger.

"Give me my own fur!" he cried, "not the fur of my cousin, turned inside out!"

"If you have a man's body, you will have to spend the winter in a man's house," Run Along told him. "Do you remember your wife?"

"She had two cubs in the spring and then went away," Bear said.

"I mean your human wife," Run Along explained.

"I have no human wife!" Bear growled. "I'm a bear!"

"Only part of you is a bear," Run Along reminded him. "The rest of you is married to Pudding Spoon. If you're strong enough to walk now, come with me."

As Run Along approached the village with Bear, he was met as before by the village dogs. Deer Button had been a favorite with them. But when they gathered around him, barking happily, he now met them with a cuff of his hand and snapping jaws. In a few moments Run Along was in the middle of a fight.

"Don't bother with them! They won't hurt you!" Run Along shouted desperately. "Come right into your house!"

Half the dogs followed them into the hall where Pudding Spoon and two other women were making corn bread and soup, with babies in their cradle boards beside them. Four children were playing on the floor.

Bear smelled the soup, lifted the pot from the fire, burned his hands and flung it into the air with a roar of pain. The dogs barked. The babies cried. The children screamed with

fright. The women fell over one another, trying to get out of the way.

"Two of you grab him!" Run Along shouted to the women. "He's too starved to be strong!"

In about a minute the longhouse was quiet enough for Pudding Spoon to speak out in anger. "What kind of creature have you brought me now?" she demanded of Run Along.

"He's the rest of your husband," Run Along explained. "I thought you would like to have him back."

But Pudding Spoon's new present did not make her happy.

"What am I supposed to do with this part," she asked, "cook ants and grubs for him? Or should I sleep in a cave with him for the rest of the winter?"

Run Along was glad that he was not married to her. She was hard to please.

Pudding Spoon threw two loaves of bread in Bear's direction. Then she and the other two women quieted the children, cleaned the floor and started to make another pot of soup. When Bear had eaten the bread, he sat quietly in a corner to lick his burned hands. Run Along went home. What would happen now? he wondered.

Nothing unusual happened. As one day passed into another, Pudding Spoon found it easier to live with a bear whose body was like her husband's than with a husband whose body was like a bear's. With a little training, Bear learned to eat with a spoon, sleep in a bed and do simple jobs like carrying wood or getting water. He liked attention. He liked to be warm instead of cold and hungry. By the second moon he was whining at other longhouses for work. At the end of the winter, he was known throughout the village as Helping Boy.

Run Along and he played the common winter games together and became good friends, so Run Along did not look forward to the warm May winds that would bring Wood Thrush flying north again. A boy thought differently from a bear. To be with a bear was fun.

The sun became stronger and stronger. The sap stirred in the maples. Then one morning Deer Button appeared in the door of his longhouse, thin and cranky, and demanded something to eat.

He was glad to find his body again, but angry to find that Bear had become a welcome guest where he was not wanted.

"As soon as Wood Thrush comes, we'll go to the magic spring and have our heads cut off and put back where they belong!" he exclaimed to Pudding Spoon.

"But suppose that the spring has lost its power, so that you both die?" Pudding Spoon asked.

"We won't do them at the same time," Deer Button said.

"We'll cut off Bear's head first. Then if he dies, you'll still have me."

"That's what I'm afraid of," Pudding Spoon said.

At last Wood Thrush's voice broke upon the morning air. Run Along, Deer Button, Bear, and Pudding Spoon all gathered eagerly under the branch on which he perched.

"If you're my friend, I demand that you give me back my rightful body!" Deer Button exclaimed. "How can I go on like this, half bear and half man?"

"Have no fear," Wood Thrush said. "The magic spring has filled the cup again. There is a risk, but I know a charm which added to the water ought to turn you into your true selves."

"Come on!" Deer Button said to the other. "I can't stand it a moment longer!"

So with Wood Thrush flying ahead from tree to tree, they all went into the forest to the spring. The cup, they found, was full. Deer Button and Bear lay down side by side. Run Along sprinkled both their heads and necks carefully. Wood Thrush sang his charm.

The two who sat up were a whole bear and a man.

Bear got to his feet, looked at his paws, and gave a little whine of pleasure. "It's been lovely knowing you," he said to Pudding Spoon. "But your husband was the one who first tried to kill me, and if I stay, he'll probably try it again. So I think I'll go on home."

Deer Button then jumped up with a happy shout. "Pudding Spoon! Pudding Spoon!" he cried, "I'm a man again!"

Pudding Spoon examined his neck to make sure that his head was secure and tight. "Very well," she said. "I'll be your wife. But if you start complaining or break your bed again, back to the woods you go!"

The Drums Call

Wolf Handle opened his eyes. What had wakened him? The longhouse was dark and silent, except for the breathing and stirring of his sleeping family. Then, breaking through these sounds, he heard the beating of drums like a command repeated again and again by his father. Where did it come from? What did it mean?

He was a dreamy, quiet boy who would rather make a bow and arrow than shoot it. He closed his eyes and turned on his side. But he could not go back to sleep. The beating grew louder. Its pace quickened. "Get up and see! Get up and see!" the drums sang. It made him afraid, as if the Evil One were calling his name.

He pulled on his leggings and stepped through the door into the night. The drums were louder there. A thin shaving of the moon lay among the pines, resting in its own soft light. A panther screamed far off and was answered by hunting wolves. He could see no drums, but their sound and the night made him shiver though he was not cold.

He wanted to go back to the safety of his bed, but he found himself walking toward the forest in time with the drums.

Soon he was running. Then suddenly the beating burst into thunder and swept him along as if he had fallen into a rapids. He ran and ran until he dropped upon the ground, exhausted, into a soundless sleep.

When he awoke, the night had turned black and lay heavily upon the earth. He was alone in a deep ravine, alone with his ears and a sad owl. He heard the drums again, nearer but not so fast or loud, as if he had done their bidding. He sat up. He stared in the direction of the drums and saw a cluster of lights coming toward him. A procession of figures slowly took form.

Who were they? And what were they doing in the night? The leader was a very old man. The figure behind him had a beaver's legs and a broad flat tail. Then came a boy and two men whom he recognized. One was Orangewood, whose gentle hands had shown him how to carve war clubs and bowls. The other was Bitter Grass, the medicine man, who had often taken him on his searches for herbs.

One by one they came to an opening and laid their torches upon the ground to form a fire. One by one they sat and became silent.

"We all know why we have come again to the ravine," the old man said. "But we must wait until we find out whom the drums have chosen."

77 THE DRUMS CALL

Two times Wolf Handle ran stumbling in the opposite direction. Two times the drums punished his ears until he returned. Then slowly he stepped into the light of the fire.

"I am here," he said.

"Enter our circle," the old man directed, "and we will tell you why we brought our torches to this place."

Wolf Handle sat down with his back to the fire.

"As you know," the old man began, "many years ago a great chief from the west, with five warriors for our one, conquered our villages. To save our children, we promised that every other year we would send presents and a man from one village to race against him for his life. No one can beat him. So in this way we have lost our strongest and swiftest men. Would you go on forever sacrificing the best of our tribe or would you think it better to send others of less worth?"

"I have heard my father say that the strongest are the most needed," Wolf Handle replied.

"And the one needed the least is he who has evil in his heart," the old man said. "Are you that one?"

"No!" Wolf Handle cried. He did not want to die. "Why have you chosen me?"

"The drums have done the choosing," the old man said. "We shall find out now whether they are right." Then his eyes went around the circle like a scout trying to find a trail. Two of the faces were stern. Two were softened with pity. "Who would like to speak first?" he asked.

The figure that was half beaver and half man slapped the ground angrily with his tail and stood up. "I would!" he exclaimed. "Everyone knows that I am a harmless creature. Working day after day with my teeth and feet and tail, I built a dam that turned a brook into a pond. Here Turtle could sun himself. Here Raccoon could fish."

"We know your value," the old man interrupted.

"But when the pond had taken form," Beaver said, "on the very afternoon my wife had given birth to our son, this boy pulled out of the dam the two logs that held it together. In the rush of water my home was destroyed and my son drowned! Why would such a boy be allowed to become a man?"

"Let him race the chief! Let him race the chief!" two voices shouted.

Wolf Handle looked at the men he knew. Did they too want him to die? When they did not speak against the others, he spoke for himself.

"Spare me, Beaver," he begged. "I didn't mean to drown your son!"

"He is dead by your hand just the same," Beaver replied. Then he took a torch from the fire. "I say that you will race the chief. Suppose I lend you speed with this?"

But before he could touch the flame to Wolf Handle's heel, Orangewood broke in. "Wait, everyone!" he said. "Beaver has given us only one taste of the pudding."

The old man turned to Beaver, "If we are to judge him, we must act with the fairness of judges," he declared, "and not torture him before we know the entire truth. Let Orangewood speak."

"The boy didn't destroy your dam in a spirit of mischief,"

Orangewood said to Beaver. "He is my pupil. I sent him out into the woods on that day to find two basswood logs of a certain age, a certain size. The only ones he found suitable for carving were those you had cut for your dam."

Then, for all to see, he held up the figure of a young beaver, carved of wood. "This he made of a bigger log," he said. "In return for your torch, I give you back your son."

"That is impossible!" Beaver exclaimed.

Orangewood put the young beaver on the ground, scattered a pinch of tobacco on the fire, and prayed in a low voice. The figure slowly became alive, went over to his father, and

touched his nose. Beaver licked his son's face—and put his torch back into the fire.

Wolf Handle relaxed.

Then the young boy, whom Wolf Handle now recognized, stood up. "I am next," he said. "His mother asked him to look after me while the rest of our fishing party took the net to another spot. But he left me sitting beside the brook and went off by himself. If my father hadn't found me in time, I would have been killed by the wolves."

The old man was silent for several moments. "This is a serious charge," he said.

Then Bitter Grass added his word in Wolf Handle's defense. "It is serious," he agreed. "But are we ourselves perfect? I have often sent him into the fields for a rare seed or plant because I knew that no one else would have more patience in searching. His main fault is that what his heart does not take with him he forgets."

"I did forget!" Wolf Handle exclaimed. "I didn't mean to leave the boy alone!"

"His mind is filled with carving," Orangewood explained. "He will be the greatest carver this village has ever known."

In the silence that followed the drums began to beat again. But they seemed to have lost their anger.

"We have told you of the sorrow that lies upon our villages," the old man said. "Do you, who are so often lost in your thoughts, have one now that will be good for us all?"

Wolf Handle stood up slowly. "Yes," he said. "I am willing to race the chief if Orangewood will give me the old knife with magic in its blade, and the rest of you will bring me wood from strong trees that will not tire."

"Thank you," the old man said. "We will see that you have what you need. We can go home now. The drums will lead you to the meeting place."

"And we will help you in your running," Bitter Grass added.

Wolf Handle was no longer afraid. In the morning, with his best knife in his hand, he carved two human legs out of an elm. He carved arms out of basswood. He cut a head from a wise old pine and a chest and stomach from an oak. Then he laid them together and breathed his own spirit into the figure he had created. With this new body he was ready for the chief.

The drums—they made an easy trail to follow. Run, run, run, they sang. And on and on and on he ran, in the light of the sun and the dark of the rain. Drum, drum, drum. Run, run, run.

Then at last the great trees faded into a distant smear upon the horizon and he saw countless men and elk running in the same direction as he. The drums led the way, taking him finally into the midst of a circle at the top of a small hill. In its center sat the chief, the largest and strangest man he had ever seen. He had antlers on his head and a long nose covered with hair. The people stood back to listen.

"Ho ho!" laughed the chief. "The men are afraid of death, so they have sent me a child! Very well. We will run to the rim of the sky and back to see whether he will grow in his running."

He turned then to the west and began to run. Wolf Handle followed. To test his speed, the chief at first trotted at the pace of a boy. Then he ran with the longer stride of a man carrying a message. Then of a warrior going into battle.

Wolf Handle kept even.

But gradually a change came over the chief. His legs grew more slender. His body grew thicker. His hair spread over his entire face. He was not a chief of men. He was chief of the elk.

Wolf Handle was dismayed. Even though his new body would never tire, how could the swiftest of men outrun an elk? He lengthened his stride, but the chief now kept well ahead.

On and on they ran and finally came to a strange land filled with huge rocks, as if a mountain had been dropped from the sky and had broken into a thousand pieces. The chief jumped over the first rock, then the second one, and disappeared. Wolf Handle ran around the first rock, then stopped. How could he race against an opponent he could not see?

Orangewood then took form at his side with a crow they had once made together. "Follow the crow," he said, letting it fly into the air. "As the crow flies is the quickest way out of this plain."

Wolf Handle thanked him and ran on.

The chief gave a snort of rage as they came out of the valley together, and he dug his hoofs into the ground to increase his speed. The boy would have to tire soon!

But Wolf Handle, with his heart of oak and legs of elm, did not tire. And the crow flew overhead to guide him whenever the chief drew out of sight.

At last on the third day the chief began to breathe hoarsely and stumble over little stones.

Then Wolf Handle found Bitter Grass running at his side. "The chief knows now that you will win the race," he said. "So he will try to kill you to prevent you from taking the news to his people. Here is a tiny dagger. Hide it in your hand. If he attacks you, plunge it into one of his hind legs. Only in that way can he be killed."

On the fourth day, the chief staggered up a small hill and

fell over on his side. Wolf Handle ran on past him to prove that he had won, then walked back to where he lay.

"You have won the race," the chief said. "Now you will be chief. If you will help me up, I will carry you home on my back."

Wolf Handle took one step forward. The chief jumped to his feet, lowered his great antlers and charged him. Wolf Handle leapt aside and buried his dagger in the chief's leg as he passed. The chief stumbled and fell over dead.

Wolf Handle sank slowly to the ground, then crawled out of his wooden body into his true self and closed his eyes. He was so tired, so tired.

But he had saved his people and could hear the drums no more.

Turtle's War Party

As Turtle lay sunning himself upon a log, he felt a sharp blow. Quickly he drew his head back into his shell and looked out over the pond. There on the shore were two Seneca boys with stones in their hands. Angrily he slid into the water and sank down to the bottom.

Did human beings think of him only as someone to throw stones at, or make rattles out of, or put into the pot for soup? Did they forget that in the beginning of the world when the Great Spirit had thrust the first woman down from heaven, there would have been no place for her to land if a turtle had not offered his broad back? He decided that the boys should be punished for their lack of gratitude. He decided to make war upon the family they belonged to and take their warm longhouse and field of corn away from them.

Where should he begin? His warriors would have to be able to fight on land as well as in the water, with weapons more deadly than the spears and arrows of the enemy.

His thoughts turned first to his friend, Beaver, who had made the pond in which they both lived by damming a stream. What sharp teeth he had! He could bite through the leg of a man as easily as through a young tree. Turtle swam over to Beaver's house and knocked on the roof.

In a few moments Beaver climbed up out of the water and joined him. He listened with approval to Turtle's plan. "I will gladly join your war party," he said. "Human beings are my enemies too."

"What have they done to you?" Turtle asked.

"Each year they have killed some member of my family," Beaver explained. "They make robes out of our fur and tools and necklaces out of our teeth."

"We will use your teeth for a better purpose than that!" Turtle exclaimed.

"I have another idea," Beaver said. "At night while they're asleep, I'll cut a hole in my dam, and the water will rush down upon their longhouse and drown them, everyone."

That was a wonderful plan! Turtle thought. And it would save him the trouble of getting other recruits.

So the very next day Beaver pulled out two of the branches that held one end of the dam together. Then Turtle and he hurried to a spot from which they could enjoy the rout of their enemy.

With a great roar, the water sped toward the house. Surely

not a person in it would escape! The water swallowed the low banks of earth. It tore up the weeds and bushes and little trees by their roots. It rushed at the door of the longhouse as if the people who had built it were its enemies too. But it could go no farther. The wise Senecas had placed their home on ground too high to be swept away by any flood.

They found that the only house damaged by the water was Beaver's own. He studied the jumbled logs with a sigh.

"Now they will go on as they did before, but *I* have no place to live. The pond will fill up again when I have repaired the dam," he said, "but you and I will both have to sleep out for a while. Do you think men are smart enough to build their houses on a high spot just so that floods won't reach them?"

"How can they be as smart as that when they can't even stay underwater more than half a minute?" Turtle asked. "It was just luck! That's what we need too. We'll go ask Rabbit's advice. Rabbits are always lucky!"

They found their friend Rabbit very sad. The same boys had caught two of his uncles in traps, and he and his cousin had just come back from the funeral.

"I would be happy to join your war party," he said. "But we rabbits aren't so lucky as we used to be."

"Nevertheless you still manage to steal their beans without

getting caught," Turtle pointed out. "We would like some ideas from you."

Rabbit was pleased to be asked for advice. He wrinkled his nose and flapped his ears to show that he was thinking. "I will get my brothers and sisters, my first cousins and second cousins, my nieces and nephews, and my children and grandchildren," he said. "Then at night we'll eat every plant in their garden —corn and squash and beans. And without food they will have to move away and leave us in peace."

"That wouldn't work," Beaver said. "They have lived here in this longhouse through good times and hard times. If we destroy their vegetables, they will only kill more of us for meat."

"I agree," said Turtle. "But Rabbit and his cousin can both help us in other ways, so I'd be glad to have them in our war party. Fox is cleverer than we. Let's go ask him the best way to fight."

"If Fox joins our war party," Rabbit objected, "the first person he will kill is me!"

"We'll make him promise not to eat any member of his own war party," Turtle said. "Besides, why should he eat you when the house is filled with delicious meat, already prepared for him?"

Rabbit finally gave in. "I will join you, but I won't invite any other member of my family," he said. "I don't trust Fox."

Then he spoke to his cousin. "You can come or not, which-ever way you think is better."

"I'll come," his cousin said. "It ought to be exciting."

When they all approached Fox's den, he quickly scratched some loose earth over the rabbit bones that lay on the ground and greeted his visitors with a very warm smile. "Welcome, my dear friends!" he said. "What can I do to help you?"

Turtle explained why they had dared come to his den.

Fox smiled. "I'll join your war party," he said, "only if you make me the chief. And you must give me the first piece of meat we find in the longhouse."

"I will make you the war chief," Turtle said, "and let you lead us in battle. But it's my war party, so I have the right to decide everything else."

"Very well," Fox said. "Then speaking as war chief, I say that we can't win unless we take them by surprise. So we must get rid of the dogs first."

"How can we do that?" Turtle asked.

"I suggest that Rabbit and his cousin run past the long-house a little ahead of us," Fox said. "The dogs will run after them, and then we can attack before the people inside can get their weapons."

"But suppose that the dogs catch my cousin and me?" Rabbit asked.

"It will be a noble sacrifice for the good of all," Fox said.

Then he spoke to Rabbit's cousin: "Let's practice now. I'll pretend to be one of the dogs."

Rabbit's cousin was from a distant meadow and too young to have had experience with foxes. "All right," he said.

He ran off into the bushes with Fox after him.

In a little while Fox returned alone, looking as if he had just eaten a big meal. "We had a very sad accident," he told the rest. "So I had to bury him."

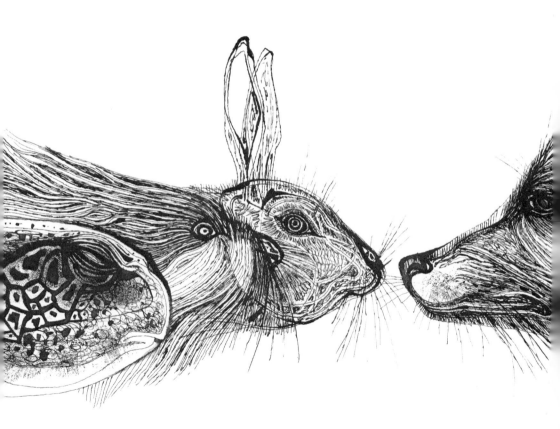

Rabbit said nothing. He suspected at once that Fox had caught his cousin and killed him. Pretending to be in search of food, he went farther and farther across the meadow and did not come back.

To make up for this loss, however, Skunk, who happened to be walking by, joined them.

Beaver then pointed out a problem. "There are twenty-one people in the longhouse," he said. "How can we attack so many?"

"The family will soon be going to their hunting camp," Fox said, "and will probably leave only the old man and woman behind. How can they defend themselves? I suggest that we find a scout who can crawl up close to the wall without being seen and discover what their plans are."

"I'll be the scout," Skunk offered. "I can crawl right up beside it at night and listen without anyone knowing I am there."

The others all laughed.

"They may not *see* you," Fox pointed out, "but everyone knows when you're within fifty paces. And please don't sit so close! I can hardly breathe!"

Skunk moved back halfway into a bush, his feelings hurt. Why did everyone complain about him? His mother had always said that he smelled *nice*!

But who would be their scout? Fox and Turtle and Beaver and Skunk all thought for a while and decided to ask Rattlesnake to take the part.

"He can crawl through any hole," Fox said. "And if he's caught, he can kill a person with one bite."

Rattlesnake said that he would be very glad to spy for them. "Human beings aren't fair!" he exclaimed. "You know I'm tenderhearted and always warn off anyone before I strike. But the moment I warn them, they attack me!"

So Rattlesnake joined the war party and proved to be a wonderful scout. He wriggled through a hole in the longhouse wall and learned that the family was going to its hunting lodge in a week. "And Fox was right," he added. "They're going to leave the two old people behind."

Turtle was excited then and invited Bear and Panther to join them. Now he had a real war party with two members who were stronger than the enemy! He also invited Otter and Mink and Crayfish and Frog.

But unfortunately, in planning the attack, Turtle had one idea, Bear another and Fox a third.

"I must be the war chief too," Turtle said at last. "The war party was my idea, so that proves I'm the smartest."

"You may be smart," said Fox, "but you can't move fast

enough to lead a war party in battle. The chief should be the one who can run the fastest."

"Then why not let a race decide it?" Panther suggested.

"We'll have a wrestling match and let *that* decide it," Bear said. "The strongest one should be our chief!"

They found that Bear, Panther, Beaver, and Fox each wanted a test that he himself would be sure to win. What were they to do?

They agreed at last to a race. Fox could run the fastest over a short distance. Bear and Panther each thought that he would win a long race. Turtle had his own plan.

"Very good," Turtle said. "Now we must vote whether the race will be on land or in the water. I vote for the water."

Beaver, Otter, Frog, Mink, Crayfish and Turtle all voted for the water. Bear, Panther, Fox, Rattlesnake and Skunk voted for the land.

"That makes six against five," Turtle announced. "We win."

Bear and Panther and Fox were annoyed to think that he had outsmarted them. But they had agreed to accept the vote.

"Now everyone line up at this end of the pond," Turtle directed, "and when I say go, we will all swim to the other side. The one to touch the other shore first will be the chief."

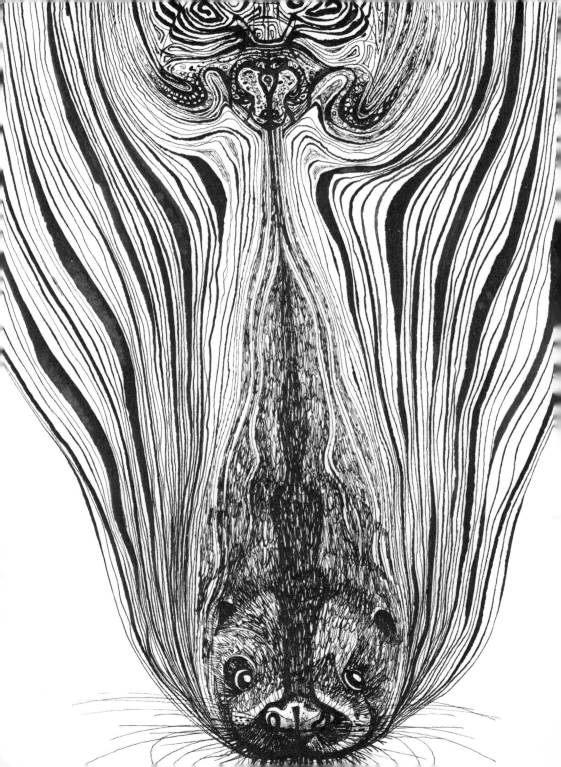

At Turtle's signal all but Fox, who did not like to get his tail wet, jumped into the water. What a splash there was! Otter was the fastest swimmer. When he leaped into the water, Turtle caught his tail in his jaws and held on. Otter could not stop to see what was making the extra weight. He swam with all his might and soon was out in front. But before he could touch the opposite shore, Turtle bit sharply into his tail. He whirled around with surprise and pain and flung Turtle through the air onto the sand.

Turtle watched with satisfaction as the rest came puffing out of the water. "I have won the race," he said. "Now I will tell you how to attack."

"I swam the fastest!" Otter objected. "I should be chief!"

"We will all agree that you swam the fastest," Turtle said calmly. "You even took a passenger with you! But you didn't reach the shore first. Besides you wouldn't make a good chief now because you're going to have a very sore tail."

The others, too, were angry. Only Fox laughed at Turtle's trickery.

"It takes more than a good swimmer to win a war," Turtle said. "I have just proved that I can get into action first."

"You cheated!" Beaver exclaimed. "I won't stay in any war party of yours a moment longer!"

So Beaver, Otter, and Frog went home. But Turtle did not care. "We need intelligence to succeed," he said. "And that includes tricks."

They all agreed then that they should invite Wolf to take the place of Beaver, who would have been very slow anyway. They agreed also to fight in a group, each using his natural weapons.

Turtle looked from one to another proudly. "I hereby declare war on the human race," he announced. "Be prepared to attack at any moment."

Then he turned to Rattlesnake. "You take a position somewhere near the longhouse," he directed, "and let us know the instant the hunting party leaves."

"All right," Rattlesnake agreed. "The war has begun!"

On the afternoon of the second day Rattlesnake saw most of the household start off on the eastern trail with two dogs following them. He slid back to the pond and gave his news to Turtle.

"How about the other dogs?" Turtle asked.

"Some of them must have gone ahead," Rattlesnake replied. "There's not one in sight!"

Turtle gathered together his war party. First Skunk took his position at the rear door of the house to prevent the enemy from escaping. Then the rest advanced. How proud and confident they were! When they came to the edge of the cornfield, however, three dogs ran out of the longhouse, growling savagely. Two of them attacked Panther, and one, the biggest, jumped straight at Wolf.

Why had they been left behind?

"Onward!" shouted Turtle. "Who's afraid of traitors!"

Mink, who at one time had nearly been killed by the spotted dog, ran for the protection of his creek. Fox ran too, but only to get out of sight. Panther had to stop advancing to defend himself. Wolf was soon battling for his life.

"Charge!" cried Turtle.

Bear, Crayfish, Rattlesnake and Turtle moved forward bravely. Then the old man inside stepped out to see what had excited the dogs.

"The fire!" he shouted to the woman. "Bring out the fire!"

Then he ran back for his weapons.

"Skunk! Skunk!" Turtle directed. "Go inside and drive them out within range!"

But before Skunk had entered the back door, both the old man and woman burst into view. Bear lunged forward. The woman threw a burning stick at him and set his fur on fire. He fled to the pond, beating his chest with his paws.

The old man aimed his arrow at Panther and shot him through the heart.

On came Crayfish and Rattlesnake and Turtle. Crayfish scuttled forward and set his pincers in the old man's moccasin. The old man did not even feel it.

Rattlesnake coiled to strike. The woman stunned him by throwing a stone at his head.

Fox darted into the longhouse through the back door, seized some venison, and ran off to his den.

Wolf fled into the protection of the forest with the dogs pursuing him.

And Turtle? Only the appearance of Skunk saved his life. Skunk came out through the door, stamped his feet and shot his fire at both the old man and woman. Now it was their turn to flee, gasping for breath. They staggered into the woods and did not come back.

Turtle looked around.

The great battle was over, and only Skunk and he, the chief, were left.

"What do you want me to do now?" Skunk asked.

With Skunk so near, Turtle could hardly breathe. "I want you to go far, far away," he said.

Then he went sadly back to his pond. There he found Bear sitting in the shallows, alive but whimpering with pain.

"Well," said Turtle with a sigh as he climbed upon his log, "human beings may be better fighters than we. But we're smarter in every other way! They can't grow fur to keep themselves warm in winter or carry their houses around on their backs!"

The Magic Suit

Two brothers lived alone with their father in a small house at the edge of a village. The older was named Short Ax because he was small and quick. The younger, who was eight years old, was named Turkey Legs because he had a coat made of turkey feathers in which he could fly wherever he pleased.

One day their father called Short Ax to his side. "The time has come," he said, "to prepare yourself for manhood. First go down to the river and build a sweat lodge. When you have taken a sweat bath and fasted, the friends who will protect you for the rest of your life will appear in your dreams."

Short Ax was happy to know that his father thought he was old enough to be accepted as a man. He ate no more food. Out of branches and bark he built a small lodge. Then he put a huge bowl of water on the floor and dropped heated stones into it to make steam. In this steam he sweated until both his mind and body felt pure and clean. Then he lay under a tree and waited for his protectors to appear.

In his first dream a black-and-yellow spider, the largest he had ever seen, crawled down the tree to his shoulder. "I have wisdom and I can make traps for your enemies," Spider said.

"When you are in trouble, call on me." Short Ax thanked him and watched him crawl slowly away.

In his second dream a mouse climbed upon his knee and spoke to him. "I will be your protector too," it said. "Go out into the world now without fear." Short Ax thanked him as he had thanked Spider. Then he returned to his home.

His father looked at his glowing body and confident face with approval. "You are now a man," he said. "It's time for you to have a wife."

"Have you chosen one for me?" Short Ax asked hopefully.

"It is the women who choose a man's wife," his father said, "and you have no mother or grandmother to choose for you. The best I can do is send you out to find one for yourself."

"I want to marry the daughter of a chief!" Short Ax exclaimed.

"Very well," his father said. "You may try. But to win her you will need better clothing than you have on now. Come into the house with me and see what I have that will fit you."

In the storage space above his bed, his father uncovered a cap of heron feathers, a soft and glossy robe of panther skin, a deerskin shirt, and leggings decorated with red and blue porcupine quills.

Short Ax put them on. They fitted as if a woman's eye had measured them. Then his father added a pouch with a magic root and a bow that looked old and crooked but would guide an arrow straight to its mark.

"No young woman can resist you now," his father said. "The heron feathers will guide you. The robe and leggings will keep you young. The root will guard you against evil. The arrows will provide you with food."

"But the bow is old and bent," Short Ax objected. "Shouldn't I have a better one?"

"Its appearance will protect it from thieves," his father pointed out. "It once belonged to the great hunter, Bear Paw. Every arrow that flies from it will reach its mark no matter where it is pointed."

Short Ax looked down at his arms and legs and bent his bow with deep satisfaction.

"Go now in these clothes," his father said, "and bring back a good wife."

Short Ax said good-bye to his father and Turkey Legs and started off on the great trail to the east. It was a long and lonely trail. But toward evening when he stopped from hunger, he was happily surprised to find that Turkey Legs had followed him through the air.

"I'm going with you," Turkey Legs said. "I will be a better protector than your bow and arrow. From the air I can warn you when danger is ahead."

107 THE MAGIC SUIT

Short Ax smiled at him. How could an eight-year-old boy protect him against a wizard or a bear? But he was glad to have his brother's company.

On the second day they came upon a crippled boy playing with acorns under a large oak. The boy greeted them in a friendly voice and asked Short Ax to put him on one of the branches so that he could swing up and down. But as Short Ax bent forward, a mouse darted out from his hole and nipped the boy's heel, so that he hobbled off crying. Short Ax recognized his protector. What danger could there be in helping a boy? He glanced up into a tree, puzzled.

"Let me look," Turkey Legs said.

He flew up above the tree and returned to where Short Ax stood, his wings quickened with fright. "There's a wizard hiding above where the boy wanted to go!" he whispered. "He has a rope in his hand to drop around your neck! We must slip away quietly!"

When they walked into view from the top of the tree, the wizard gave a scream of rage at having been outwitted. Then he turned into a weasel and ran into a hole in the tree.

Short Ax and Turkey Legs went on. Late in the afternoon, when the sun was donning its war paint, they came to a trail lodge in a grove of elms. Under one of the elms an old man was limping about.

"Look!" he exclaimed, pointing to a branch on the largest tree. "There's a fat raccoon, but I have no bow and arrow with which to shoot him. Shoot him for me, so that I can eat!"

"Gladly," said Short Ax, taking his bow from his shoulder.

"No!" whispered Turkey Legs. "Wait!"

But surely there could be no harm in shooting a raccoon for an old man, Short Ax thought. He aimed at the raccoon and pierced its chest with his arrow. The raccoon ran to the trunk, climbed to a large hole and disappeared inside it.

"Now you have lost it for me!" the old man cried. "It has gone into its hole to die, and I'm too old and weak from lack of food to get it!"

"You haven't lost it," Short Ax said. "I'll catch it and throw it down to you."

"Oh, no, no!" the old man objected. "You would spoil your beautiful new clothes! Take them off first. I'll watch them for you."

Short Ax took off his robe and shirt and leggings and gave them to Turkey Legs. Then he climbed the tree. But when he reached the hole, he found it much deeper than he had thought. He thrust his head and shoulders inside and stretched out his right arm.

Suddenly the old man climbed up the trunk like a squirrel

and shoved him into the hole. Down he fell into a mass of rotting wood and bones. Too late he realized that he had been trapped by the same wizard Turkey Legs had discovered in the tree. He could hear Turkey Legs gobbling in the air. Then there was silence.

That night in a dream filled with horrors a mouse with a black-and-yellow head like a spider's appeared before Short Ax and reminded him of his protectors. He woke up and lay quietly for a moment with the beginning of hope.

"Mouse, Mouse," he whispered, "if you can help me even against magic, come and help me now!"

Mouse did not appear or speak. But soon afterward Short Ax heard a gentle gnawing halfway up the trunk. Then a tiny nose pushed a piece of rotted wood free from the trunk and enlarged the opening into a hole. Short Ax tried to catch hold of its edge and pull himself up. But it was too high for him to reach.

"I can't make a hole farther down," Mouse said. "The wood is alive and too thick."

Short Ax then thought of Spider. "Spider," he called, "I need both my protectors tonight!"

A moment later Spider appeared in the hole. There he spun and wove until he had made a rope of silken threads, all braided together. When he had let it down, Short Ax took hold of it and pulled himself up to Mouse's hole. He could see the moon! He was free!

"Oh, thank you both!" he said. Then he broke off more of the rotted wood until the hole was big enough for him to crawl through easily and he slid to the ground.

At his feet lay his bow and arrow and the wizard's dirty ragged clothes. Where had he gone? What had happened to Turkey Legs?

"Turkey Legs," he called, "are you here?"

Turkey Legs flew down from the limb on which he was sleeping and greeted him happily. "The old man must be the same wizard who was going to hang you!" he said. "He stole your clothes and left you his old rags!"

Short Ax picked up the bow and arrow. "At least he left my bow," he said. "He must have thought it was too old to be of any use."

"I managed to escape into the air," Turkey Legs explained. "Then I followed him. There's a large village not far away. When he put on your clothes and started toward it, he changed into a handsome young man. He went straight to the chief's longhouse, and asked to marry his daughter."

"What happened then?" Short Ax asked anxiously.

"I lit on the roof near a smoke hole where I could hear,"

Turkey Legs explained. "By the time he got there, he looked like the son of a chief, so the chief and his wife gave their consent."

Short Ax was angry at himself. Why hadn't he been more careful?

"Then we'll have to go on to another village," he said.

"There's a younger daughter," Turkey Legs informed him. "Perhaps she will marry you."

"We can try," Short Ax said. "At least we must warn them of their danger."

When Short Ax had put on the wizard's dirty shirt, torn leggings and stiff moccasins, he found that he could not straighten out his shoulders or hold up his head. Did the clothes of the wizard have magic power too? He tried to take off the shirt, but could not. It seemed to be glued to his skin.

"I'll have to go as I am," he said unhappily. "What young woman will marry me looking like this?"

As Turkey Legs and he set out, every step weakened him and made him look older. When they came to the river that separated them from the village, they looked like a man of seventy and his grandson.

On the other side of the river, they saw a young woman standing beside a canoe.

"Will you help us across the river?" Turkey Legs shouted.

113 THE MAGIC SUIT

They could not hear her reply. But she pushed the bow of the canoe into the water and paddled across to the spot where they were standing.

"Welcome to our village," she said. "My name is Trillium."

Short Ax loved her the moment he heard her voice. She was as fresh and beautiful as the flower she was named for.

"Are you by any chance the daughter of the chief?" he asked.

"Yes," she replied. "I am one of two. My sister was married yesterday to a stranger like you."

"I also have come to find a wife," Short Ax told her.

"We are glad to have you as our guest," Trillium said. "But I am the only unmarried woman in the village and I don't want to marry an old man."

"He's not old. He's my brother," Turkey Legs informed her. "He was bewitched on the way by the stranger who just married your sister. The man is a wizard. No member of your family is safe as long as he is alive."

As Trillium paddled back across the river, Short Ax told her how the wizard had imprisoned him and stolen his clothes. She was frightened by his tale, but she found it hard to believe that any suit could have the power to make an old man young again.

"I will prove that my suit has magic power," Short Ax said,

picking up his bow. "The wizard left my bow, thinking that it was useless because it was old and bent. But it has the same power as my robe and leggings. Hold up your paddle and watch."

Trillium took her paddle out of the water and held it upright. Short Ax shot an arrow in the opposite direction. It circled a willow tree, returned, and pierced the center of the paddle.

Trillium pulled out the arrow. "I believe you," she said.

"Somehow I must get my clothes away from the wizard," Short Ax said. "Will you help me?"

"Yes," Trillium agreed. "My sister is in danger as long as he is her husband."

She beached the canoe and took Short Ax to her father, the chief. The wizard was smoking beside him. "I have brought my husband home," she said.

At once the wizard spoke up. "Surely you won't let your daughter marry a sick old man who can't even hunt his own food!" he exclaimed.

The chief did not like to be advised by others. "I think my daughter is wise enough to make a good choice," he said.

Trillium and Short Ax thanked him. Then Trillium helped Short Ax to the part of the longhouse where she kept her possessions and showed him the fragrant bed covered with soft deerskin robes where they were to sleep. She made another bed in the storage area for Turkey Legs.

That evening Short Ax ate the marriage bread and became Trillium's husband. He had thought that it would be easy to get his clothes back once his enemy had gone to sleep. But the wizard kept both his robe and leggings on all night.

What were they to do? Was he to be an old man for the rest of his life? Suddenly he remembered his protectors.

"Mouse, Mouse," he prayed, "I need all your cunning!"

With a tiny squeak Mouse came up out of a hole in the bark wall. "How can I help you?" he asked.

"I want you to bring me the root that's in the pouch the wizard stole from me," Short Ax explained. "Then my magic will be stronger than his."

"I will try," Mouse agreed. "But if he should feel his pouch move, he would catch me and crush me to death. I must have help from Spider."

Short Ax summoned his protector.

"I'll sew up his eyes so that he can't see," Spider offered.

"That will save us all," Short Ax said.

Late that night Mouse and Spider crept up into the wizard's bed while he was asleep. First Spider bound his eyelids together with his silk. Then Mouse pulled the root gently out of the pouch.

The wizard felt the movement of his pouch, but he was unable to open his eyes to see what had caused it.

"Thief! Thief!" he shouted.

His wife woke up. But Mouse was already out of sight.

"Someone has blinded me!" the wizard exclaimed. "Catch him or we are ruined!"

"You are having a nightmare," his wife said. "There is no one here." Then she went back to sleep.

Mouse ran with the root to where Short Ax was waiting.

"You and Spider are true friends," Short Ax said, accepting the root gratefully.

With the root once again in his control, Short Ax had little fear of the wizard. The following afternoon he gathered the people together in an open place and challenged him to a contest.

"We will dance, one after the other, you and I," he said, "and see which of us truly has a young heart and lungs. To make it fair, we'll both wear the same moccasins. Lend me yours for a moment."

The wizard refused.

The chief spoke up then. "Give him your moccasins," he said. "If you are what you claim, it can do no harm."

The wizard still refused. Then Short Ax took off the wizard's own moccasins and pointed the root at them. "Go

find the feet you were made for," he commanded.

In an instant the old moccasins were on the wizard's feet and the new ones on his own. He began to dance. He danced the feather dance. He danced the war dance and ended with a great leap over the nearest longhouse. Through it all he breathed as slowly and quietly as a young man. The people marvelled and began to believe.

"Now let the thief who has stolen all my clothes dance!" Short Ax said to the chief with scorn.

Again the wizard refused to take part. But now the people jeered at him.

"You must answer Short Ax's charges or leave our village!" the chief said.

The wizard stood up. But with his own moccasins on he could only limp a few feet. His legs had suddenly become thin and weak.

"Now give me my suit!" Short Ax demanded.

"Never!" the wizard cried. "You will be an old man as long as you live!"

The wizard summoned a panther out of the air, climbed on its back, and went leaping off through the trees. But before he could get out of sight, Short Ax drew his bow and shot an arrow in his direction. For all to see, the arrow flew here and there like a dog trying to find a trail, then sighted the wizard and pierced his heart.

At once both the wizard and the panther disappeared. Short Ax ran forward. Upon the ground lay his robe, shirt and leggings. Inside the shirt there was nothing but an old giant puffball that smoked to the touch.

Short Ax put on his clothes and returned to the group, looking his true age once again. Trillium ran to his side with delight.

"It was hard to believe what you told me," she said. "But now it has all come true!"

"You have probably saved our village from some great evil," the chief said. "We welcome you for as long as you want to stay."

About the Author

"Writing is my life," says Roger Squire. "I began at the age of 18 with short stories, wrote a novel about my youth, and finally switched to playwriting which has been my true love ever since." One of his plays has been produced by the Studio Theater in Buffalo, New York, and another for the United States Steel Hour.

Until 1958, Mr. Squire was the Curator of Education at the Albright-Knox Art Gallery, in Buffalo. He is now a Research Consultant for the Buffalo and Erie County Historical Association. The author has always had an avid interest in the Iroquois Indians and this is his first book about them for children.

About the Illustrator

Charles Keeping is a noted British artist whose acclaim is growing steadily in the United States. His graphics have been exhibited extensively in England and on the continent.

Among the many books Mr. Keeping has illustrated for children are THE KING'S CONTEST AND OTHER NORTH AFRICAN TALES; THE SKY EATER AND OTHER SOUTH SEA TALES; POKO AND THE GOLDEN DEMON; and FIVE FABLES FROM FRANCE.

S